This book belongs to

Ella Sherwood
....
from your godmother,
Olivia ♡

Written by Tim Bugbird.
Illustrated by Nadine Wickenden.

The love in my heart

Tim Bugbird

Nadine Wickenden

make
believe
ideas

Big and Boo were resting,
after bouncing in the forest all day.
They were a long way from home
and Boo was very tired.

"I don't think I can make it all the way back to the burrow," said Boo. "My paws are just too sore!"

Big smiled and took Boo's hand.
"Well, I know **you can**,
and do you know why?"
said Big.

"Because with love in our hearts, we can do anything!"

As they walked, Big began to explain...

The love in our hearts could scent every flower.

The **love** in our *hearts* could cloak every tree.

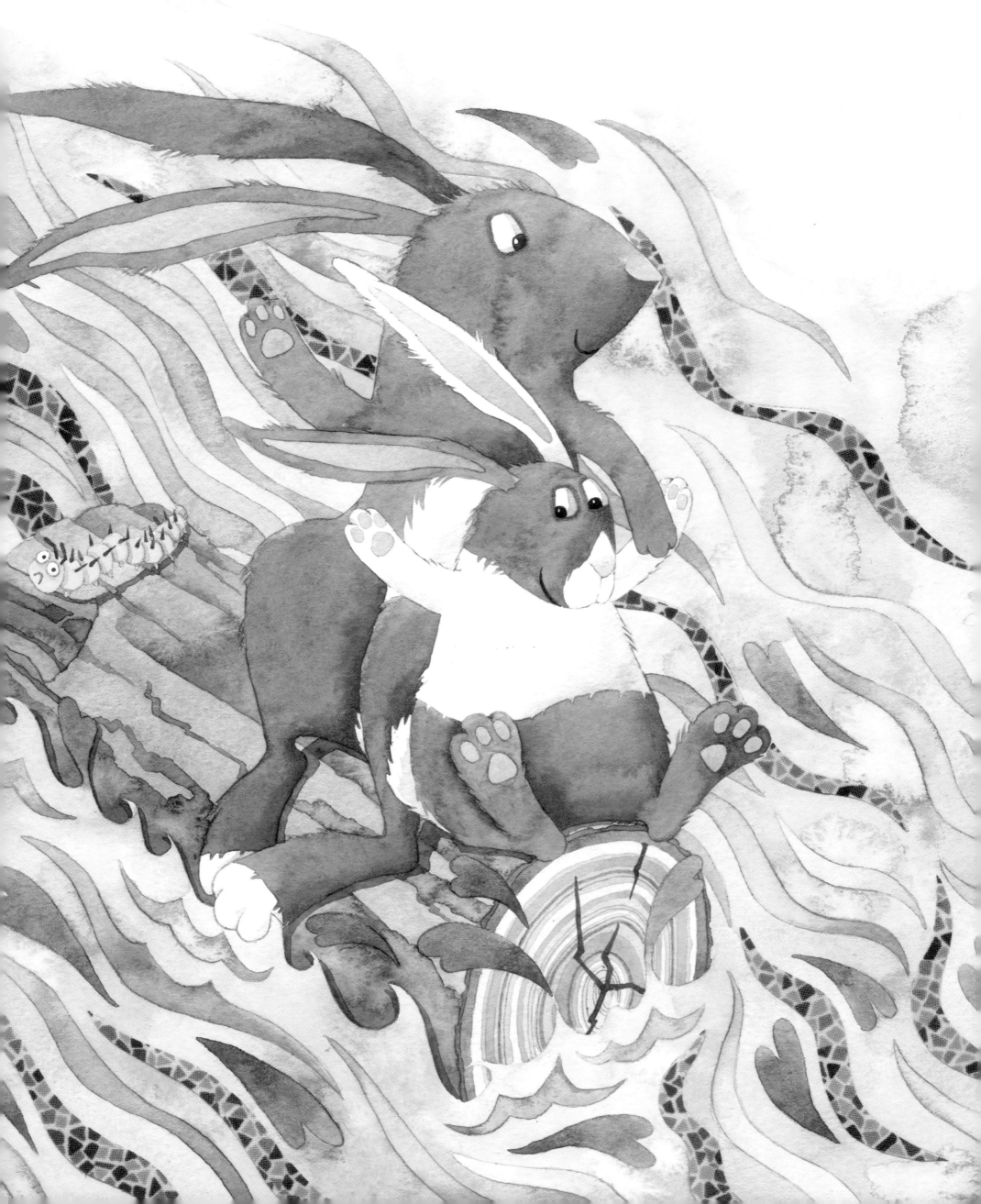

There's no doubt in my mind,

we could fill every river

with ripples of love,

all the way to the sea.

The love that we share could color a

rainbow,

with plenty left over
to **light up** the sky.

And the **love** in our **hearts** could cap every mountain with soft, **snowy blankets** of **caring** piled high.

The **love** in our **hearts**
could change thunder to **song,**

and carpet a **pathway**,
no matter how long.

The love in our hearts could turn gray skies to blue.

With **love** we can do anything,
just **me** and **you!**

And before they knew it,
Big and **Boo** were home,
snuggled up in their cozy burrow.

"I love you," whispered Big.
But Boo was sound asleep.